A Handful of Seeds

Monica Hughes

paintings by Luis Garay

ORCHARD BOOKS
New York

Text copyright © 1993 by Monica Hughes
Illustrations copyright © 1993 by Luis Garay
First American Edition 1996 published by Orchard Books
First published in Canada by Lester Publishing Limited in 1993

LIBRARY OF CONGRESS CATALOGING-IN-PUBLICATION DATA
Hughes, Monica.
A handful of seeds / Monica Hughes ; paintings by Luis Garay. —
1st American ed.
p.   cm.
Summary: Forced into the barrio by her grandmother's death,
Concepcion takes with her a legacy of chili, corn, and bean seeds
and finds that they hold the key to her survival.
ISBN 0-531-09498-7
[1. Seeds—Fiction. 2. Gardening—Fiction. 3. City and town
life—Fiction. 4. Grandmothers—Fiction.]   I. Garay, Luis, ill.
II. Title.
PZ7.H87364Han   1996   95-20850

Orchard Books
95 Madison Avenue
New York, NY 10016

Manufactured in Hong Kong

10 9 8 7 6 5 4 3 2 1

For my friends in Development and Peace, and for all the children
M. H.

With all my love, for Ana and Rene Garay
L. G.

Concepcion lived with her grandmother in a little house on a hill. Together they cleared the stones to make a vegetable garden. They planted corn and beans and chilies.

"Remember to save enough seed for the next planting," Grandmother said. "Then you will always have something to eat."

Every day Concepcion walked to the stream to get water and walked back with the heavy cans hanging from her shoulders. Carefully she poured the precious water around the corn. Weeks passed. The sun shone. Later the rain came and the corn grew tall. The beans wound around their stalks to reach the sun. The chili bushes flowered.

When the corn and the beans and the chilies were ripe, Grandmother gave some to the man who owned the land, saved some to eat, and sold the rest to the neighbor who took it to sell in the city far away in the valley below. He brought back fresh buns and rice for them to eat.

One sad day, Grandmother died.

"You cannot stay here," said the man who owned the land. "I have a family ready to move in."

"But I will work for you," said Concepcion.

"This family can work harder and grow more corn and beans," he said. So she had to leave the little house with its painted walls and clean mud floor.

"Come and live with us," the neighbor's wife said. But Concepcion knew she already had seven children to feed.

"I will go there." Concepcion pointed to the misty valley where the city lay.

"It is a long walk for such little legs." The neighbor's wife shook her head.

"My legs are strong from carrying water." Concepcion said good-bye and hugged the neighbor's wife and all the children.

"God go with you," they all said.

Concepcion bundled up the corn, beans, and chilies that Grandmother had saved and set off with her cart down the stony path into the valley. It was a very long walk and Concepcion's bare feet were tired and sore by the time she reached the *barrio* on the edge of the city.

She saw hundreds of huts made of tin and plastic and cardboard, crowded close together, each leaning toward the next. "Is *this* the city?" Concepcion wondered in dismay. "I thought it would be beautiful."

She walked along the narrow muddy paths, stumbling with tiredness until she bumped into a gang of children.

"Look where you're going, can't you?"

"I ask your pardon," Concepcion said politely.

Their clothes were torn and their faces were dirty and their hair tangled. But when she smiled at them, they smiled back.

"My name is Tomas. Where are you from?"

Concepcion pointed to the far hills. "But my grandmother is dead."

"Stay with us. We will teach you how to pick garbage and sell it, and how to take food from the merchants' stalls without being seen."

"That is stealing," said Concepcion, surprised.

Tomas shrugged. "It is better than starving."

"I have corn and beans and chilies."

"That's not enough for one good meal," said Tomas scornfully.

"When they grow, there will be enough. You will see."

"You're crazy. They'll never grow here. But you can stay with us."

So Concepcion lived with the children on the edge of the dump. She dug the hard ground with the broken handle of a kettle. She made a tiny wall of stones and she planted some of her corn and beans and chilies.

Every day she watered them and watched them grow, until they came up green and bright. The beans and the chili bushes flowered, the prettiest sight in the whole *barrio*. Concepcion was sure that her dear grandmother was watching over the little garden.

But one day Tomas and the others came running around the edge of the dump with the police chasing after them. The police yelled and hit her friends with their sticks. The children screamed and cried.

Concepcion hid among the garbage. "Why did I come to the city?" she asked herself. When everything was quiet, she peeked out, like a frightened mouse. The children were covered with bruises and the garden had been trampled flat.

"Why are you crying?" Tomas asked crossly. "The police didn't beat you."

"My garden is spoiled. If the corn and beans and chilies had ripened, we would have food to eat and sell, and you wouldn't have to steal."

"No use crying. It's all finished now."

Concepcion dried her eyes. "I have some seeds left."

Tomas licked his cut lip and nodded. "This time we will all help you plant your corn and beans and chilies."

With everyone's help they dug a big plot and planted the rest of Grandmother's seeds. They took turns watering them and guarding them. Soon the corn grew high and the bean pods were fat and firm and the chilies were green and shiny.

"We'll have a feast," said Tomas. "And take the rest into the city to sell."

"But we must always save enough seeds to plant," Concepcion reminded him.

They cooked the corn and beans with chilies. The delicious smell of food soon filled the air. As they began to eat, another hungry gang of children appeared. Concepcion and Tomas and the others shared their meal with them.

"But our garden cannot feed all the children in the *barrio*," Concepcion said sadly.

Suddenly she had an idea. She took some of the seeds she had saved and gave them to the leader of the other gang. She told him how to make a garden, how to plant and water the seeds.

"Always save enough seeds for another planting and to share with other children," she told him, as Grandmother had told her. He promised he would do so.

Concepcion was sure that Grandmother was smiling down on her from the sky, and that her eyes were no longer misty with age but as bright as the stars that shone over the *barrio*.